Copyright © 2020

make believe ideas ltd

The Wilderness, Berkhamsted, Hertfordshire, HP4 2AZ, UK.
501 Nelson Place, P.O. Box 141000, Nashville, TN 37214-1000, USA.

www.makebelieveideas.com

Written by Alexandra Robinson.
Illustrated by Clare Fennell.

THE UNICORNS

are coming to town

Clare Fennell ★ Alexandra Robinson

make
believe
ideas

One bright and merry *Christmas Eve*,
Santa planned a treat.
He booked the *Unicorn Ice Spa*
for his faithful *reindeer fleet*.

Excitedly, they went inside
to start their *pamper day.*
They dressed in gowns and fluffy socks,
then dashed to the *buffet.*

The **unicorns** were mega fans
of *Santa's reindeer crew*.
So having them as special guests
made all their *dreams* come true.

They welcomed in the **VIPs**,
greeting them with awe,
then served them up their *buffet feast*,
with snacks and treats galore.

Throughout the day, the *reindeer team*

were *pampered* to the *max.*

This is
the life!

Hoof Shine Station

Glitter

They chilled out in the *tinsel tub*,

with snow masks to *relax*.

Inside the *Ice Spa Hair Salon*,
they had a snow shampoo.

You look
deer-vine!

Their fur was dried and *styled* with *gems*,
plus *bells* and *baubles*, too!

And though the *jewels* were *everywhere,*
the *deer* kept wanting *more.*

Soon their coats were so *bejeweled,*
they couldn't see the floor!

Before long, **Santa's sleigh team** had to leave for Christmas Town.

These jewels weigh a ton!

Hope to see you soon!

The glitzy **reindeer** called their jet and packed their dressing gowns.

The **reindeer** knew the *unicorns* would love to watch their *flight*.

They said: "We've got some extra seats — come join us for tonight."

When the *unicorns* arrived,
the *elves* gave them a tour.
They marveled at the *toy parade*
and giant *chocolate store*.

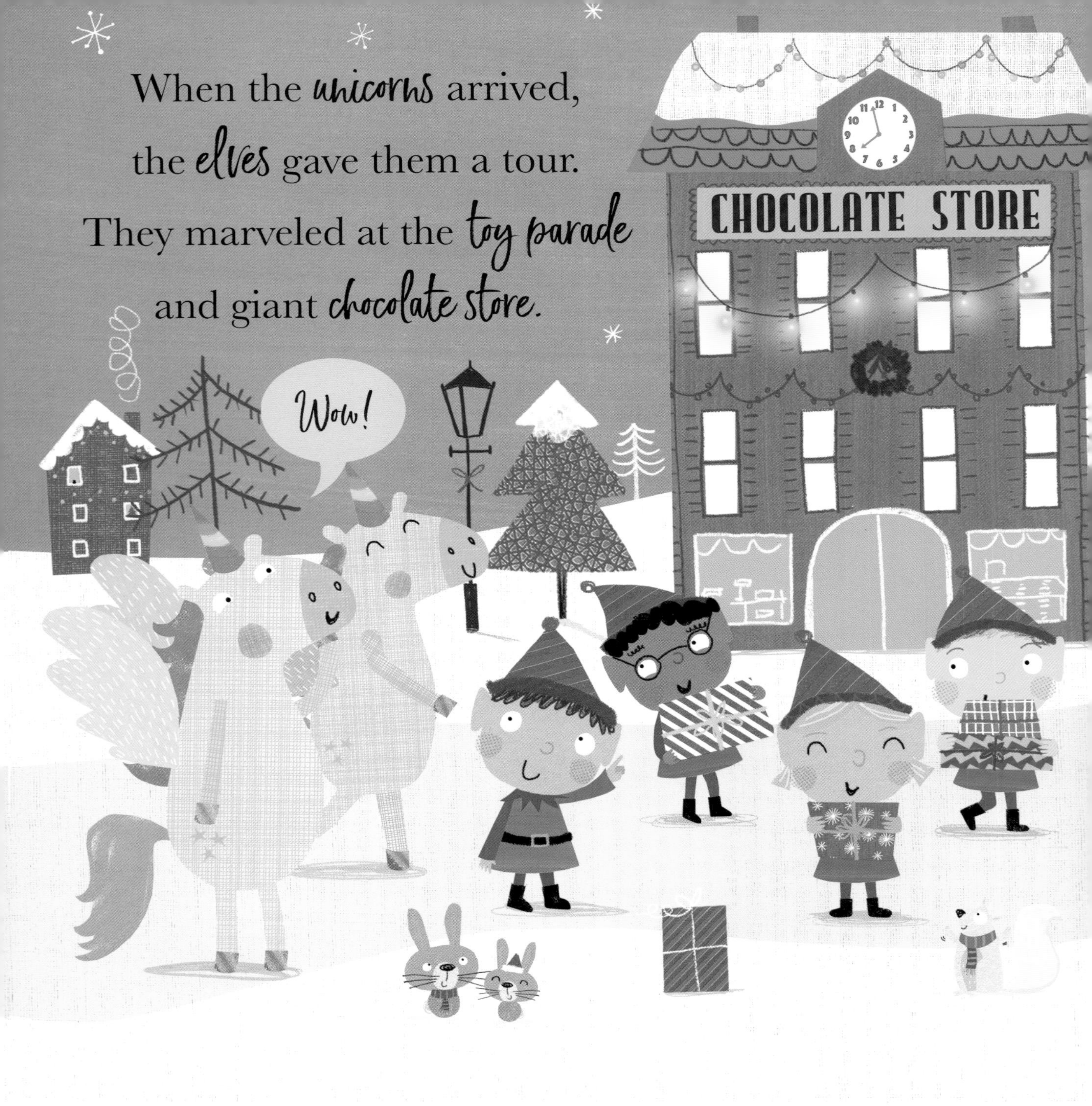
CHOCOLATE STORE
Wow!

The clock struck eight, and it was time
for *Santa's team* to go.
So everybody **marched** uphill
to watch the *Sleigh Launch Show.*

But when the *deer* put on their reins,
the *straps* began to *break*,
and the extra *jingly-jangly bells*
just made their poor heads ache.

And as they jumped for takeoff,
their jeweled coats weighed them down.
They howled,

"We'll never pull the sleigh –
we can't leave Christmas Town!"

Ouch!

The elves and snowmen tried to help
with tiny combs and tools.
But all the bells were stuck in place,
and so were all the jewels!

The reindeer team felt helpless, but then one cried out with glee;

"The unicorns could fly the sleigh, if they will all agree!"

That's a good idea!

The *unicorns* looked doubtful –
they'd *never flown* a sleigh.

"You can do it," said the deer.
"Trust yourselves today!"

The brave, excited unicorns all nodded with delight:

"We'll try our best, and use our horns to guide you through the night."

The reindeer clapped with joy and said:
"You've saved this Christmas Eve!"
Then Santa and the unicorns
prepared the sleigh to leave.

From far and wide, the crowds appeared
to see the big reveal
of Santa's jazzed-up Christmas sleigh . . .

. . . with a *rainbow steering wheel!*

They *flew* to every single town and *galloped perfectly,*
delivering *gifts* around the world, as *happy* as could be!

Happy Christmas,
one and all!

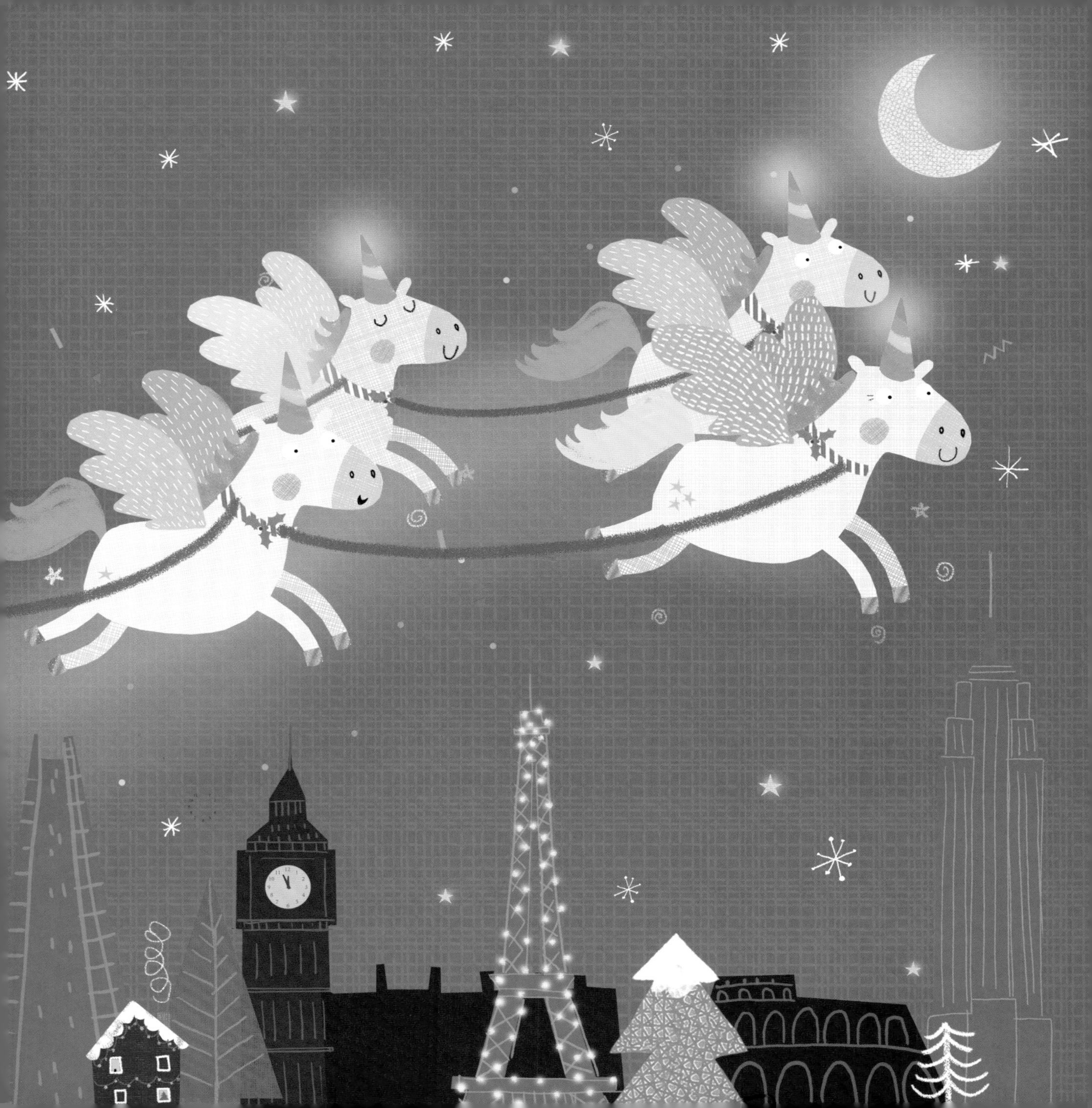

The next day, all the **unicorns** received a *gold rosette*.

They'd won a **North -Pole record** for the *fastest* sleigh ride yet!